DISNEY'S
THE
LION KING

Adapted from the film by Gina Ingoglia

DISNEY PRESS

New York

1

The moon had vanished. One by one the stars faded from the cold night sky. Behind the dark eastern hills, the sun rose, turning the flat-topped acacia trees from black to green. Once again, it was dawn in Africa.

This was an important day.

"Hurry," the animals urged one another. "Today's the day we go to Pride Rock. We can't be late!"

Up from the wide valleys and down from the hills, they paraded across the plain. Cheetahs, the fastest of all, led the way. The dusty ground shook beneath a million drumming hooves and the plodding feet of the elephants and the rhinos. Silent giraffes, followed by their gangly babies, loped alongside herds of excited zebras. At the rear, troops of chattering baboons carried their alert youngsters on their backs.

The air was crowded and noisy with the flap and flutter of countless wings. Birds of all sizes and colors, flying from faraway rivers and trees, shaded the backs of the traveling animals.

The trip was long, and as the animals approached Pride Rock, the plain shimmered in the morning heat. Everyone assembled at the foot of the mountain and waited.

"When are we going to see the new prince?" a young giraffe asked.

"Soon," his father said.

From the back of the throng an ancient baboon slowly made his way to the foot of Pride Rock. Supporting himself on his walking stick, he carefully climbed the face of the mountain.

"That's Rafiki, the great mystic," an elephant explained to her child. "When King Mufasa was a cub, Rafiki watched out for him. Now he has come to give little Simba his blessing."

A blue-feathered hornbill glided down from the summit of Pride Rock. "Look, here comes Zazu," the elephant mother said, pointing with her trunk. "He's checking to see if we're all here."

Zazu circled low above the crowd a few times. Then he flew back to the top of the rock, disappearing from the sight of the patient gathering.

He landed at the feet of a dignified golden-maned lion.

"King Mufasa," Zazu reported, "everyone's arrived, and Rafiki is already on his way up. The elephants are here, and the wildebeests, as well as the—"

"Thank you, Zazu," said Mufasa. "That will do."

In a few minutes Rafiki's shaggy gray head appeared at the edge of the rock. King Mufasa embraced his old friend.

"There!" said Rafiki. "I have made it with hardly a scratch." He looked around. "Now, where's the young lad?"

Mufasa smiled and nodded toward his mate. "He is over there with Queen Sarabi," he answered.

"Here is Simba," said Sarabi, gently handing the spotted cub over to Rafiki. The cub looked up and blinked at the strange old baboon.

Rafiki grinned toothily at Mufasa. "It's as if I'm seeing you as a cub all over again.

"Now, little prince, I will give you my blessing," he said, and patted Simba on his head.

Rafiki slowly untied a gourd from his walking stick. He leaned over and shook it several times above the watchful cub. Then he cracked the gourd open, removed something sticky, and smeared it on Simba's forehead. The cub wrinkled his nose.

"Almost finished," the elderly baboon said kindly. He scooped up a handful of dust and sprinkled it over Simba's back. Simba sneezed, and they all laughed.

Then Rafiki stooped down and, with great care, gathered up King Mufasa and Queen Sarabi's son. He carried the cub to the edge of Pride Rock.

The crowd below had been waiting eagerly for this moment.

"There he is," one of them shouted. "Rafiki's holding the new prince!"

At once everyone cheered and stamped their feet.

"Welcome!" they shouted. "Welcome to Prince Simba!"

Rafiki waited for the dust to settle. Then he raised Simba high in the air. The clouds parted, and a shaft of sunlight broke through, shining down on the future king. The animals fell silent and bowed.

Rafiki slowly lowered his arms and took Simba back out of sight.

As the afternoon sun began its descent in the western sky, the animals turned to make their way home.

* * *

Later that afternoon Zazu flew to a shaded part of Pride Rock and landed at the feet of another lion—the king's younger brother.

"It gives me great pleasure to announce the visit of King Mufasa," said Zazu. "And you'd better have a good excuse for missing this morning's ceremony."

"Ooo—I quiver with fear," said Scar calmly.

"What was that?" asked Mufasa, suddenly appearing. "Sarabi and I didn't see you at the presentation of Simba. Is anything wrong?"

"That was today?" asked Scar, pretending to be disappointed. "Oh, I feel simply *awful*. Must have slipped my mind."

"You should have been first in line," scolded Zazu. "After all, you're the king's brother."

"I *was* first in line—until the little hairball was born," Scar snorted, then padded away.

"Don't turn your back on me, Scar!" ordered Mufasa.

Scar spun around and faced his brother.

"Oh, no, Mufasa," he growled. "Perhaps *you* shouldn't turn your back on *me*."

"Is that a challenge?" demanded Mufasa.

Without answering, Scar quickly retreated.

Zazu tried to ease his master's frustration. "There's one in every family, sire," he said, "and they always manage to ruin special occasions."

"What am I going to do with him?" Mufasa muttered under his breath.

2

The days passed quickly for Simba. There was so much to learn and to do. One morning before sunrise when it was still dark and chilly, he trotted over to his sleeping father and gently nudged him.

"Dad," he whispered eagerly into Mufasa's ear. No answer.

Simba spoke a little louder. "Hey, Dad. Wake up, Dad!"

Mufasa sighed in his sleep and turned over.

"Dad-Dad-Dad-Dad-Dad," Simba pressed on.

Sarabi sleepily opened her eyes.

"Your son is awake," she said to her mate.

"Before sunrise, he's *your* son," Mufasa grumbled.

Sarabi nudged him hard. "You told him to get you up early this morning."

Mufasa's eyes popped open. "I know. I'm up. I'm up."

Sarabi reached out, pulled Simba close to her, and licked his face and ears.

"Your father has some important things to tell

you today," she said. "So you'd better have clean ears."

"Mo-om," said Simba, wiggling free.

In the dim light Mufasa and Simba strolled far across the Pride Lands. All over the plain, dainty tan-and-white gazelles, busily wagging their tails, nibbled on the grass. As Mufasa and Simba passed by, they scattered, leaping stiff-legged, kicking their heels behind them.

A glowing orange ball appeared on the eastern horizon. The sun was beginning a new day. Its heat burned away the morning mist, and Simba felt the ground warming beneath his feet. The sun's long rays reached far out, sweeping across the plain, bringing light to the land.

"Look at the rays of the rising sun, Simba," the king told him. "Everything the light touches is our kingdom."

Simba was impressed. "That's just about everywhere!"

"A king's time as ruler rises and falls like the sun," his father said. "One day the sun will set on my time here. It will rise with you as the new king."

"And this land will be mine?" asked Simba.

"Everything," said Mufasa.

Simba blinked and scanned the bright plain. Small, agile mongooses, nearby, popped in and out of abandoned termite mounds. Out along the sunny horizon thirsty zebras slowly walked in single file to a crowded water hole. But far to Simba's left, the land was hazy and still.

"What about that shadowy place?" he asked.

"That's beyond our borders," said Mufasa. "You must never go there, my son."

Simba tried not to act disappointed. "But I thought a king can do whatever he wants."

His father smiled. "There's more to being king than getting your way all the time."

"Do you think I'll be a good king, Dad?" Simba asked.

Mufasa grew serious and looked into his son's eyes. "You will be a good king if you remember this: Everything you see exists together in a delicate balance. As king you need to understand and preserve that balance. You must respect all creatures—from the crawling ant to the leaping antelope."

"But we *eat* the antelope!" said Simba.

"Yes, we do," said Mufasa. "Let me explain. When we die, our bodies become the grass. Then the antelope eat the grass. And so we are all connected in the great Circle of Life."

"Good morning, sire!" a voice squawked down to them. It was Zazu. The hornbill landed in a heap at his king's feet. "I have the morning report."

"All right, Zazu," said Mufasa. "Let's hear it."

Zazu cleared his throat and began to speak in an official voice: "The buzz from the bees is that the leopards are in, well, a bit of a spot. . . ."

Simba was bored. A butterfly flitted past him, settling on a tiny flower growing close to the ground. The cub pounced, and the butterfly quickly flew away.

While Zazu droned on, Mufasa bent over and whispered to Simba. "What are you doing, Son?" he asked.

"Pouncing," said Simba. "But I missed."

Zazu paused and waited.

"Go on, Zazu," said Mufasa.

Zazu cleared his throat again and went on. "The baboons are going ape. Of course, the giraffes are acting like they're above it all. . . ."

"Let an old pro show you how to do it," Mufasa quietly said to Simba while Zazu recited his report. "Zazu, would you turn around?"

"Of course, sire," replied Zazu. With his back to the king, he continued. "The tick birds are picking on the elephants. I told the elephants to forget it, but they can't."

"Remember, Simba," Mufasa whispered to his son, "stay low to the ground."

"And the termites, as usual," reported Zazu, "are boring, boring, boring. . . .

"Uh, what's going on?" he asked, glancing behind him.

"Don't worry," answered Mufasa. "Just a little lesson in pouncing."

"Oh, very good," said Zazu, turning back around. Simba was only pouncing. POUNCING?

"Try not to make a sound," Mufasa instructed his son.

Simba, crouching low, made his way toward Zazu.

"Sire," protested Zazu over his shoulder. "You can't be serious. This is humiliating. For me to be so degraded—"

A muffled scrambling sound stopped the indignant hornbill in midsentence. An exhausted mole poked his head out of a small hole in the ground. Bleary-eyed and sneezing dust, he quickly whispered in Zazu's ear and disappeared again.

"Sire, there's news from the underground," said Zazu. "Hyenas have been spotted crossing into the Pride Lands."

Mufasa looked concerned. "Zazu, take Simba home while I look into this," he said, starting to leave.

"Let me go with you—please, Dad," Simba begged.

"No," the king called back. "It could be dangerous."

Zazu escorted Simba back to the foot of Pride Rock.

"Thank you, Zazu," said the cub. "I can go the rest of the way myself."

He left his father's secretary and scrambled up the rocky ledges. Halfway to the summit, he came across Scar, snoozing on an overhanging rock. The thin lion opened one eye. It was half covered by a scraggly black mane.

"Oh," he said, looking down at Simba. "It's just you."

"Uncle Scar!" cried Simba. "Guess what?"

"I despise guessing games," said Scar.

"I'm going to be king of Pride Rock!" announced Simba.

Scar yawned. "Oh goodie," he said. "Well, forgive me for not leaping for joy. Bad back, you know."

"My dad just showed me the whole kingdom," Simba said. "And someday I'll rule it all!"

Scar's other eye popped open while he thought this over for a minute. "So your father showed you the whole kingdom, did he?"

"Everything!" said Simba.

"He didn't show you what's beyond the northern border?" asked his uncle.

"Well, no," said Simba. "He said I can't go there."

Scar yawned again. "And he's absolutely right. It's far too dangerous. Only the bravest of lions go there." He closed his eyes. "Now go away and let me get a little shut-eye."

"Uncle Scar," said Simba. "*I'm* brave! Please tell me what's out there."

"No," said Scar firmly, keeping his eyes closed. "I'm only looking out for your well-being. An elephant graveyard is no place for a young prince."

"An elephant *what*?" asked Simba. This sounded interesting.

Scar opened his eyes wide. "Oops!" he said with a grin. "Oh dear, I've said too much. But you're so clever, I'm sure you'd have found out sooner or later. Just do me a little favor, will you? Promise me you'll never visit that dreadful place.

"And don't tell anyone I told you," he added. "It will be our little secret."

"Sure," said Simba.

He ran off to find his best friend, Nala. He couldn't tell her *how* he knew, but he could tell her *what* he knew!

14

3

S imba played with Nala almost every day. They climbed trees together, wrestled, and raced across the plain. Now he couldn't wait to tell her about the elephant graveyard!

He heard his mother's voice and found her visiting Sarafina, Nala's mother. They were resting in the shade of the kigelia trees behind Pride Rock. Sarafina was giving her impatient daughter a bath.

"Hold still—*please*, Nala," she scolded. "Let me finish washing your face. Just a couple more licks and you can go."

"Hi, everybody," said Simba.

"Be with you in a minute," said Nala. "I *hope*."

While he waited, Simba played with the heavy sausagelike fruits that fell from the trees.

"How was your walk?" Sarabi asked her son.

"Fine," said Simba. "Dad had to go and check on some hyenas. They've come onto our lands."

Sarabi was startled. "Really? Again? I hope he runs them off. Those hyenas are nothing but trouble!"

"Can Nala come out and play?" Simba asked Sarafina.

15

Sarafina looked at Sarabi. "Do you think it's safe," she asked, "with the hyenas running around loose?"

Sarabi thought about it. "Well," she said, "it's all right with me as long as Zazu goes with them."

Simba's shoulders slumped. "Please, Mother," he begged. "Can't we go alone?"

"We're both getting pretty big," said Nala.

"And strong!" added Simba, puffing out his chest.

"Not today," said Sarabi. She scanned the top of the kigelia trees and spotted Zazu settling down for a nap.

"Zazu," she called. "I'd like you to keep an eye on Simba and Nala this afternoon."

Zazu blinked. He was *supposed* to be off duty! Oh well. He flew down to the ground. Simba and Nala strolled over to him.

"Step lively," said Zazu. "The sooner we go, the sooner we can return."

"Yeah," Simba said. "We'll run on ahead."

The two cubs scampered out onto the plain, talking and giggling.

"Where're we going?" asked Nala.

"An elephant graveyard," answered Simba.

Nala's eyes grew big. "Really?" she asked.

"Shh," said Simba, slowing down and whispering. "Zazu . . ."

"Right," Nala nodded. She whispered back.

"How're we going to ditch the dodo? Watch out, here he comes."

"Well," said Zazu, fluttering above them. "Just look at you two telling secrets. Little seeds of romance blossoming in the savannah. It's so perfect, being that you're betrothed and all."

"Be-*what*?" asked Simba. "What's that?"

"You and Nala are betrothed," sang out Zazu. "Intended! Affianced!"

"Huh?" said Simba and Nala.

"It means," explained Zazu, "one day you two are going to be married!"

"Married!" said Simba and Nala. "Us?"

"You!" said Zazu.

"I can't marry Nala," said Simba. "She's my friend."

"Right!" agreed Nala. "We don't want to get *married*."

"Sorry to burst your bubble," said Zazu, "but you two turtledoves have no choice. It's all been settled by your parents. It's an old tradition that goes back generations."

"Well, we'll just see," said Simba. "When I'm king, that'll be the first tradition to go. Come on, Nala, I'll race you to that big termite mound."

The two cubs dashed away.

"Oh dear, they're off again," said Zazu. "Wait for me!"

4

W hen are we going to get there?" asked Nala, running neck and neck with Simba. "We passed that termite mound ages ago."

"Soon, I hope," said Simba. "I just used that termite mound as an excuse to get away from Zazu."

Nala stopped running and stretched out on the grass. "Well, I need a rest."

Simba trotted over to her. "Come on, get up. I bet we're almost there."

No answer. Simba leaned over and looked at Nala closely. Her eyes were closed, and her tongue was hanging out.

"Nala," asked Simba, "are you okay?"

Nala sprang to her feet and threw Simba to the ground.

"Pinned ya!" she said playfully.

"Hey, let me up!" cried Simba.

Nala released her hold.

"Listen, Nala," Simba said, getting annoyed. "Stop kidding around. We have to get going. . . ."

Nala leapt forward and knocked Simba to the ground.

"Pinned ya again!" she cried, and dashed off laughing.

Simba ran to catch up. After a few minutes he looked behind them. "Good," he said. "We've lost Zazu."

"Where are we?" asked Nala. "Look at this place. There're no trees or anything. And the air looks all misty. It's really creepy."

"Yeah, let's go check it out!" said Simba.

"Simba, what's that weird rumbling sound?" said Nala.

Simba stopped and listened. The sound was coming from under the ground. "Gosh," he said, "I don't know. . . ."

The sound grew louder and louder. *WHOOOOOSH!* With a gigantic blast, a gush of steam exploded into the air.

"Look out!" shouted Simba.

They were both thrown off their feet, and they landed several yards away.

"What was *that*?" gasped Nala. She wiggled her legs to make sure she was still all in one piece.

"Ow!" said Simba. His back hurt; he'd been thrown against something hard. After the steam cleared he saw what it was. He was looking into the empty eye socket of an enormous elephant skull!

Simba was delighted. "This is it!" he cried. "This is the elephant graveyard!"

"Wow! This is great!" said Nala. "Look at all these bones."

"Let's get a good look at this skull," Simba suggested.

He started to climb inside. "Hey, there's something in here."

"Just one minute!" squawked Zazu, coming in for a landing.

Simba looked up, startled. Then he smiled weakly. "Oh, hi, Zazu."

"You must leave here *immediately*!" demanded Zazu. "This is way beyond the boundary of the Pride Lands. And right now we're all in very real danger."

"Danger? Ha!" boasted Simba. "Watch me laugh in the face of danger." He tossed back his head and laughed loudly.

Just then other voices laughed—from inside the elephant skull! Simba, Nala, and Zazu backed up. Giggling like mad, three drooling hyenas climbed out to greet them.

"Hyenas!" gasped Zazu. "We're done for!"

A foul-smelling hyena with a filthy mane sniffed the air. "Well, well, well, Banzai," she said to one of her companions. "What've we got here?"

Banzai chuckled. "I don't know, Shenzi," he said. "What do *you* think, Ed?"

Ed giggled. "Hee-hee-hee!"

"That's just what I was thinkin'," said Banzai. "A trio of trespassers."

Zazu nervously whispered to Simba and Nala. "Try to leave quietly," he instructed them, "while I do the talking.

"I assure you," he explained to the hyenas, "we've arrived here purely by mistake. We were just on our way out."

Shenzi circled around Zazu for a closer look. All at once something dawned on her. She reached out and grabbed him by the neck.

"I know you," she said. "You work for Mufasa!"

"I, madam," Zazu announced with pride, "am the king's personal secretary."

Banzai circled around Simba. "And that would make you . . . ," he began.

"The future king," said Simba. He stood as tall as he could.

Shenzi released Zazu, who fluttered over to stand between Simba and Nala. Then the hyena smiled, showing her sharp, dirty teeth.

"You know what we do to kings who step out of their kingdom?" she asked Simba.

"You can't do anything to me," said Simba.

"Oh, but they can," Zazu said under his breath. "We *are* on their land."

"But Zazu," said Simba. "They sneak onto our land all the time!"

"What I meant was," said Shenzi, "we'd love to have you stick around for dinner."

"Sure," added Banzai. "We can eat what's *lion* around."

Ed snickered.

Banzai made a grab for Simba's tail.

"Wait a minute, Banzai," said Shenzi. "*I'm* having the lion cubs. You grab the bird."

"Oh no you don't," Banzai argued. "I haven't snacked on cub for years. *You* grab the bird, and *I'll* grab the cubs."

"Oh no you don't," Shenzi said. "*You* get the bird, and *I'll* take the cubs. . . ."

"Come on," Zazu muttered to Simba and Nala. "Let's sneak out of here while they're fighting."

Simba and Nala quietly backed away. As soon as they were out of sight, they ran.

Ed saw the cubs go. Frantically he tried to let Shenzi and Banzai know. But they were too busy arguing to notice.

"All right! All right!" said Banzai. "We'll split the bird."

"I get the wings!" cried Shenzi.

"Oh *sure*," said Banzai. "And *I* get stuck with the bill."

"Okay, okay," said Shenzi. "We'll split the bill."

Suddenly Ed poked his nose between them and started gesturing wildly.

"What, Ed, what?" yelled Shenzi.

"Hey," cried Banzai, seeing the cubs in the distance. "Did we order this dinner to go? 'Cause there it goes!"

"After them!" shrieked Shenzi.

5

Still running hard, Simba glanced back over his shoulder. Good! No one in sight.

"We made it!" he shouted to Nala. "We made it, Zazu! Zazu? Nala, where's Zazu?"

Nala stopped to catch her breath. She cocked her head and listened.

"Do you hear that?" she asked. "The hyenas are laughing hysterically—maybe they've caught Zazu!"

"We'd better go see!" said Simba.

"No need for that," said Shenzi, suddenly appearing. "We're right HERE!" Ed was right behind her, giggling.

"Simba!" Nala screamed.

Simba took a hard swipe at Shenzi, forcing her back, and yelled, "RUN, NALA!"

As the two cubs raced back toward the graveyard, Simba spotted an enormous pile of bones.

"Quick," he said. "Let's try to climb over it."

As they scrambled up the pile, Banzai's head poked out from between the elephant bones. "Boo!" he said.

Simba and Nala backtracked in a hurry and

bumped right smack into Shenzi and Ed.

"You two going somewhere?" asked Shenzi.

The cubs skittered between her legs and dashed up another pile of bones.

"Watch out," Simba warned Nala. "It's really shaky up here."

Just as he spoke they both lost their footing and fell.

Nala gasped—they'd landed inside a giant rib cage.

"We're trapped!" she said to Simba.

Shenzi and Banzai, giggling, sauntered up to them.

"How convenient, Banzai," said Shenzi. "Which snack do you want?"

Simba felt his heart beating wildly. Maybe he could frighten them with a roar. After all, he'd heard his father do it enough times. He took a deep breath.

"Rrrr," he squeaked.

The three hyenas broke into frenzied laughter.

"That was it?" said Shenzi. "Come on, do it again. Come on, kitty, kitty, kitty," she taunted.

Simba took another deep breath.

"ROAAARRRR!"

The three hyenas spun around. They looked straight into the furious eyes of a huge lion.

"It's King Mufasa!" gasped Shenzi. "Quick,

guys!" she said to Banzai and Ed. "Let's get out of here!"

Mufasa roared again, and the hyenas fled howling into the mist.

"Dad," Simba said, trying not to cry, "am I glad to see *you*!"

"You have disobeyed me," Mufasa growled.

Simba had never heard his father sound so angry.

"I'm sorry, Dad, really," he said.

Before Simba could say anything else, Zazu limped up to them. His feathers were battered and tangled and his bill slightly bent.

"Zazu!" cried Simba and Nala.

"Good gracious, man!" Mufasa exclaimed. "What happened to you?"

"Sire," explained Zazu, "I feel simply awful about all of this, but I must point out—"

"It's not your fault, Zazu," said the king. "Now, will you please escort Nala home. I've got to teach my son a lesson."

Mufasa waited until he and his son were alone.

"Simba," he said, "I'm very disappointed in you. You could have been killed. And what's worse, you put Nala in danger. Not to mention what happened to poor Zazu!"

Simba felt terrible. He'd let his father down—his father, who meant the world to him!

"I was just trying to be brave like you," he tried to explain.

Mufasa stared at his trembling son. It made his heart ache to think what could have happened!

"I'm only brave when I have to be," he said gently.

"But you're not scared of anything," said Simba.

"I was today," said his father. "I thought I might lose you. Just remember, being brave doesn't mean you go looking for trouble." Then he smiled. "Now, let's go home—it's getting late. Your mother's worried about you."

The sun was setting. As soon as it slipped beyond the distant purple hills, the air felt cold. A full moon appeared, and stars twinkled in the blackening sky.

"Dad," said Simba, trotting alongside the king. "We'll always be together, right?"

Mufasa stopped. "Simba, let me tell you something my father told me. Look at the stars."

Simba gazed upward.

"The great kings of the past look down on us from those stars," said his father.

"Really?" asked Simba.

"Yes," said Mufasa. "So whenever you feel alone, just remember that they'll always be there to guide you—and so will I."

Simba nodded. "I'll remember."

* * *

Not far away, Scar was meeting with the hyenas.

"I told you a hundred times, boss—we're sorry!" Banzai said to the king's angry brother.

"I practically delivered those cubs to you!" Scar snarled. "You had a perfect opportunity to get rid of that little pest Simba."

"What were we supposed to do?" asked Banzai. "Kill Mufasa?"

"Precisely," Scar said.

Shenzi's jaw dropped. "Are you kidding?" she asked.

Scar grinned at her.

"I guess not," said Shenzi. "Who needs a king, anyway."

"Yeah, who needs a king," echoed Banzai.

"You idiots!" scoffed Scar. "There will be a king—me! And if you stick with me, you hyenas will be treated well. Very well indeed."

"Sounds good to me," said Banzai.

"Now listen, you mongrels. I have a little plan," Scar whispered.

The hyenas leaned in and listened. Then Shenzi and Banzai smiled broadly at each other. Ed threw back his head and laughed.

6

The next morning Simba followed Scar to the bottom of a wide, deep gorge. The cub cautiously picked his way down the jagged rocks. Every now and then, he tripped.

"Careful, my little one," Scar said sweetly. "We don't want you to fall, do we!"

"Where're we going, Uncle Scar?" asked Simba.

Scar didn't answer. When they reached the bottom he led his nephew to a flat rock in the middle of the gorge.

"Hop up!" he said. He prodded Simba onto the rock. "Wait here; your father has a marvelous surprise for you." He turned to leave. "Now I'll just go tell him that you're ready."

Simba was restless. "I'll go with you!"

"Just stay on the rock," Scar insisted. "You don't want to disobey your father and end up in another mess like you did yesterday—with the hyenas."

"You know about that?" asked Simba.

"Simba, my boy," replied Scar, "*everyone* knows about it. And just between us—you might want to work on that little roar of yours." Scar loped away and left his nephew all alone.

"Little roar—huh!" said Simba. He centered himself on the rock and drew a deep breath. "Rrrr . . . RRrr . . ." Simba stopped roaring when he heard the mournful honking sounds of wildebeests in the distance. After a few minutes he noticed a large herd of wildebeests moving along the top of the ridge. He sighed impatiently; what was keeping Dad?

* * *

Shenzi, Banzai, and Ed waited for Scar's signal.

"Where is he?" Banzai asked, peering down into the gorge. "I'm so hungry. . . . I just gotta have a wildebeest. They're coming this way. If he doesn't hurry, they'll be gone. The whole plan will fall apart."

"You know we have to wait until Scar gives us the sign," said Shenzi. "*Then* we can make our move.

"Look!" she yelped. "There's Scar. There's the signal—let's go!"

Whooping wildly, the hyenas chased after the unsuspecting wildebeests, nipping sharply at their heels. The startled animals bellowed and began to stampede.

"Drive them down into the gorge!" Shenzi yelled to her comrades.

"What do you think I'm trying to do?" coughed Banzai, spitting out dust.

A few minutes later Ed laughed hysterically as the herd veered toward the rim of the gorge.

"There they go!" yowled Banzai. "We did it!"

At that moment Mufasa was taking his usual stroll along the top of the gorge. Zazu, perched on his master's back, was reporting the news of the day.

"Look, sire," he pointed out with one of his wings. "The herd is on the move; they're coming this way."

"That's odd," noted Mufasa. As he watched the frenzied wildebeests, his brother, Scar, ran up to him.

"Mufasa!" he shouted. "Quick! A stampede! Simba's down there!"

"I'll fly ahead," cried Zazu.

Mufasa lunged toward the edge of the gorge. "Tell my son I'm coming!"

* * *

Simba watched as the wildebeests poured down the side of the gorge. There were thousands of them—and they were heading right at him! Wildly scrambling down from the rock, he ran for his life.

Before he knew it, the stampede was practically upon him. The noise of the hooves was deafening, and the dust was so thick that Simba could hardly see. But, ahead in his path, he dimly made out the outline of an enormous ancient baobab tree. If he could just reach it before he got trampled to death!

Running so fast that he thought his heart would burst, Simba reached the baobab and clawed his way up the ribbed trunk. He crawled out onto a wide, sturdy-looking limb.

"Simba!" squawked Zazu. He flew through the blinding dust and landed on top of the tree. "Hold on—your father's on the way!"

Simba leaned back to see Zazu. As he shifted his weight, the limb creaked and started to break off.

"Zazu!" screamed Simba. "Help me!"

Zazu squinted through the dusty air and saw Mufasa battling his way through the herd of wildebeests.

"He's over here, sire!" he shouted.

SNAP! The old limb broke, and Simba fell to the hard ground. Mufasa grabbed his son in his mouth. Dodging his way through the stampeding animals, he managed to get Simba up onto a rocky ledge on the side of the gorge.

"Oh, Dad," sobbed Simba. "You came just in time."

A galloping wildebeest knocked Mufasa from

The great mystic Rafiki arrives at Pride Rock to anoint King Mufasa's young cub.

King Mufasa nuzzles his mate, Queen Sarabi.

The animals of the savannah gather to pay homage to the future king.

Behold the newborn prince—Simba.

Mufasa's jealous brother, Scar, surveys the land
that he believes should be his. He'll do whatever
it takes to be king.

Zazu, the king's faithful secretary, tries to keep
young Simba out of trouble.

Scar's snickering hyena henchmen, Shenzi, Banzai, and Ed, get ready to provoke a wildebeest stampede.

Simba finds temporary refuge on a tree branch as the angry stampede charges below.

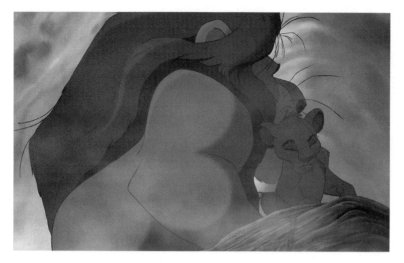

Mufasa rushes into the fray to rescue his son.

Mufasa struggles to hang on to the rocky cliff
after being injured by the galloping herd.

Scar gives the fatal push that sends Mufasa to his
death.

Timon tries to help his friend Pumbaa out of a
tight spot.

Nala stalks through the grass at the edge of the
jungle.

Rafiki finds Simba in the jungle and urges him to
return to Pride Rock.

King Scar inspects his hyena troops.

With the Pride Lands wasting away under Scar's fiendish rule, Simba knows he must reclaim the throne.

the ledge. The king fell backward and was swept away by the stampede.

"Dad!" cried Simba. "Dad!"

* * *

Several minutes later Mufasa managed to pull himself up toward the top of the gorge. Injured and in pain, he clung to an overhanging rock. Slowly he looked up to see his brother poised above him.

"Scar—help me!" he cried.

Scar leaned over and dug his claws into Mufasa's front legs. Then, with a deadly push, he whispered, "Long live the king."

Mufasa slid down the steep, jagged incline and was still.

Scar looked down from the rim of the gorge and grinned. One down and one to go. It was too bad that Mufasa had rescued Simba, but his nephew would be taken care of soon enough.

He squinted. Was that the little fellow now? It was. Simba was running across the bottom of the gorge. He'd spotted Mufasa lying in the trampled dirt.

By the time Scar reached him, Simba was sobbing next to the dead king.

"Dad," whimpered Simba. He buried his face in his father's dusty mane.

"Simba," demanded Scar, "what have you done?"

"It was an accident," Simba wailed. "He came to save me."

Sadly Scar shook his head. "If it weren't for you, he'd still be alive."

"But I didn't mean it, Uncle Scar," said Simba.

"Of course you didn't," said Scar. "No one ever means for these things to happen. But the king is dead. And you can never show your face in the pride again."

Simba looked up wide-eyed. "What am I going to do?"

"Run away, Simba!" said Scar. "Run away and never return!"

He watched his nephew run, sobbing, down the length of the gorge. Shenzi and Banzai ambled up behind Scar.

"Nice work," said Banzai. "You got rid of him."

"Now finish the job," ordered Scar, still staring after Simba. "Kill him—now."

* * *

Scar strode triumphantly to Pride Rock. As soon as he arrived he called Sarabi and Zazu to appear before him.

"I have dreadful news," he told them. "My dear brother, Mufasa, and my cherished nephew, Simba, are dead."

"No . . . no . . . ," moaned Sarabi.

Zazu was too stunned to speak. He tried to

pull himself together to console his queen.

"I'm so sorry," he said gently. "Is there anything I can do for you?"

But the weight of the news had crushed Sarabi, and she slowly sank to the ground.

"You must take comfort that your husband died a hero," said Scar. "It is with a heavy heart that I assume the throne. However, we must never forget the great Mufasa and his beloved son."

The lionesses of Pride Rock heard Sarabi's cry of grief, and they rushed to her side. When they learned the news, their wails echoed across the plain.

By nightfall thousands of animals had journeyed to Pride Rock. Their last visit had been one of joy to welcome the new prince. This time they came in grief, mourning his death and that of his father.

Atop a high ridge, Rafiki shook his head. Then, brokenhearted, the old baboon wandered off to be alone.

When Rafiki reached his home, he approached a familiar painting on the inside of the hollow tree. For a long, silent moment, he gazed at the image of the lion cub, then sadly ran his hand over it.

7

Simba stumbled across the dry, cracked earth. Thank goodness the hyenas had stopped chasing him! They had turned back after getting stuck in a mass of thornbushes.

But before the hyenas had abandoned the chase, Simba had heard them scream after him: "If you ever come back—we'll kill you!"

Simba sighed. They probably thought he couldn't make it out here on his own, anyway. And they were right.

He was exhausted and very thirsty. The air was so hot that the plain shimmered before his eyes. There wasn't a tree in sight. If he didn't find some shade and a water hole soon, he'd pass out. But, really, he didn't care if he lived or died. If it hadn't been for him, his father would still be alive.

Simba took a few more shaky steps. A shadow passed overhead, and he looked up. In the bright white sky huge vultures slowly circled above him. His knees buckled, and he fainted.

The hungry birds descended toward Simba.

Silently they gathered around and bent over him.

"Eeeeee-yaaaa!" cried a high voice.

A fat brown warthog, with a skinny meerkat perched on his back, charged toward the surprised vultures.

"Eeeeee-yaaaa!" shouted the meerkat again. "Get out, get out! Stinkin' buzzards!"

The startled vultures scattered, then took off.

The meerkat hopped off and tiptoed cautiously over to Simba for a closer look.

"All right," he chattered, "what do we have here?"

Standing on his hind legs, the meerkat carefully lifted Simba's limp paw and examined it. After a minute or two he dropped it in alarm.

"Good grief," he croaked to the warthog. "It's a *lion*! And he's alive! Run, Pumbaa—but first, wait for me!" He clambered back onto the warthog. "Let's go, go, go!"

But Pumbaa didn't run. Instead he strutted over to take a look for himself. Squinting to see better, he peered down at the cub.

"Aw, Timon," he snorted, "it's just a little lion. Look at him. He's so cute and all alone. Can we keep him?"

"Pumbaa," Timon whispered in his companion's ear, "we're talking about a lion. Lions eat guys like us!"

"But he's so little," insisted Pumbaa.

"He's going to get BIGGER!" pointed out Timon.

"Maybe if he gets to know us, he'll be on our side," suggested Pumbaa.

"That's the stupidest thing I ever heard," snorted Timon. Then he scratched his head. "Havin' a lion around to protect us might not be such a bad idea after all."

"So we're keepin' him?" asked Pumbaa.

"Of course!" said Timon.

Pumbaa knelt down on his front legs and scooped Simba up with his snout. Carefully balancing the cub behind his tusks, he got to his feet.

"Easy does it," said Timon. "We've got a long walk ahead of us. Try not to drop him!"

* * *

Later that day Simba opened his eyes and blinked. A warthog and a meerkat were leaning over him.

"Here, open up," said Timon. He poured some water into Simba's dry mouth. "Are you okay?"

"I guess so," answered Simba. He felt much better.

"You nearly died," said Pumbaa. "We saved you."

"Thanks a lot for your help," said Simba. "But I have to go now." He got to his feet and started to walk off.

"Where're you going?" asked Timon.

Simba paused and sighed. "Nowhere."

"Pumbaa," Timon said under his breath, "I think our little lion here is depressed.

"Come back," he called to Simba. "Tell us where you're from."

"It doesn't matter," said Simba. "Nothing matters anymore."

"Sounds serious," said Timon. "Did you do something bad?"

"Not just bad," said Simba. "Something terrible. But I don't want to talk about it."

"That's all right," said Pumbaa kindly. "You don't have to."

"That's right," said Timon. "Put your past behind you. Forget it. *Hakuna matata!*"

"What?" said Simba.

"*Hakuna matata,*" Timon repeated. "It means no worries, no responsibilities. That's our philosophy."

"Why don't you stay here with us?" asked Pumbaa.

Simba thought it over. Why not? He had nowhere else to go. And it would be nice to have somebody to talk to.

"I will," he said. "Thanks."

He looked around, really seeing the place for the first time. It wasn't anything like the open plain. Here everything was leafy and grew close together. Lots of trees—very tall trees—shaded the ground, making it cool under his feet. And high in the branches, red-tailed monkeys and noisy parrots searched for fruit and nuts.

"Where are we?" asked Simba.

Timon was surprised. "You've never been in the jungle before?" he asked. "Well then, welcome to our humble home." He pushed back a huge feathery fern next to him.

Simba peeked in and saw a comfortable-looking spot on the ground, covered with palm leaves. Blooming flowers, woven among twisted vines, brightened up the place.

"It's beautiful," he told them. "Do you live in there all the time?"

"We live where we want," said Timon. "We do what we want. You know how it is—we lead the good life. By the way," Timon asked him, "are you hungry?"

"I sure am," said Simba. Things were really looking up!

"Well then," said the meerkat, "we'll find you something to eat."

Timon and Pumbaa carefully searched the jungle floor. Finally, they stopped before a heavy fallen log.

"This looks like a good spot to find some grub,"

said Timon. "See if you can budge it, Pumbaa."

Pumbaa got down on his knees and, grunting, shoved the log with his snout. Timon felt around under it and grinned.

"Good," he said to Simba as he hopped up on Pumbaa's snout. "Enough for all of us."

Simba stared at Timon's upturned paw. In it was a squirming, fat worm.

"What's that?" he asked, stepping back.

"I told you—a grub," said Timon. He popped one into his mouth. "You're a meat eater; try one. They're tasty."

Simba wrinkled his nose. "Eeewww."

"Go on," urged Pumbaa. "You'll learn to love them."

"Tastes like chicken," added Timon.

Simba took a deep breath. He was really hungry, and there didn't seem to be much of a choice. He picked up a grub and chewed it.

"Well, what do you think?" asked Timon.

"Slimy, yet satisfying," said Simba, surprised at himself.

Timon smiled. "See! You'll love it here in the jungle. Just remember our problem-free philosophy—*hakuna matata*!"

"Right," said Simba. *"Hakuna matata."*

8

Days, weeks, and months turned into years. Simba had just about grown up. The spots on his coat had faded long ago. A mane was growing around his head and shoulders.

One night he sat with Timon and Pumbaa under the stars. He liked his friends and the jungle well enough, but it wasn't the sort of life he wanted. Something was missing. *Hakuna matata* just wasn't working for him.

"Do you ever think about what those things are up there?" asked Pumbaa.

"I don't think—I know," said Timon matter-of-factly. "They're fireflies stuck in that bluish black thing."

"Oh," said Pumbaa. "I thought they were big balls of gas, millions of miles away. What do you think they are, Simba?"

Simba was lost in his own thoughts, remembering his father's long-ago words:

The great kings of the past look down on us from those stars. They'll always be there to guide you—and so will I.

"Hello, over there," persisted Timon. "Simba, couldn't you just look at the sky forever?"

Simba didn't answer. He could just imagine what his father would think of him now. He sighed so deeply that his breath scattered a wispy puff of milkweed into the air.

A sudden wind sprang up. It carried the milkweed over the treetops, far out across the plain, and into the waiting, outstretched hand of Rafiki, the old mystic.

The old, wise baboon examined the seeds. Then he hobbled into his cave and studied the painting of a lion cub he'd once drawn on the wall.

Rafiki broke open a gourd and removed something sticky. He smeared it around the cub's head. Now the painting changed. It was no longer of a cub but of a lion with a golden mane.

"It is time," Rafiki said smiling. And he prepared to leave.

* * *

The next day Pumbaa was helping Timon hunt for bugs. They weren't having much luck.

"We'll find some faster," said Timon, "if we divide up. You go this way and I'll go that way."

"I'd rather go that way and you go this way," said Pumbaa. "But if you *really* want to go that way, I can go—"

"Stop!" interrupted Timon. "Just go some way!"

43

Pumbaa trotted up to a whistling thornbush. Maybe he'd find some ants on it. He sniffed around the prickly branches—just as he'd thought!

"Timon!" he woofed. "Over here!"

He heard a twig break behind him and turned to face his friend. "I found a whole lot of ants—"

Pumbaa froze. The hairs bristled on the back of his neck, and his tail stood up straight. It wasn't Timon, after all. It was a lioness—and she looked hungry.

"TIMON! HELP!" he squealed. Frantic, he dug himself under a big fallen log and got wedged in halfway.

Timon came running. "Pumbaa?" he asked, looking at his friend's thrashing hind legs. "What are you doing under there?"

"She's gonna eat me!" screamed Pumbaa.

"Who's *she*?" asked Timon. Then he saw the lioness—and she was about to leap straight at him! Terrified, Timon shut his eyes. But nothing happened. He peeked out of one eye just as Simba shot from the bushes and tackled the lioness. They rolled over and over, grunting loudly.

"He's got her!" squealed Timon, skipping around on his hind legs. "Oh no! She's got him. Wow! He's movin' like a champ. See, Pumbaa—I told you he'd come in handy! Get her! Bite her head!"

All of a sudden the lioness flipped Simba on

his back, pinning him down with her paw.

Simba looked at her closely. "Nala?"

"Simba?" asked the lioness.

Timon watched in shock as Simba and the newcomer pranced about, roaring in delight.

"Hey, what's goin' on here?" asked Timon.

"Nala, you look great!" said Simba. "What are you doing here?"

"What do you mean what am *I* doing here?" asked Nala.

"I thought you were dead!"

"Nope," said Simba. "Here I am."

"It's so good to see you," said Nala.

"I repeat," Timon interrupted, "WHAT'S GOIN' ON HERE?"

"Timon," said Simba, "meet Nala. She's my best friend."

"Friend!" snorted Timon. "She tried to eat us."

"Sorry," said Nala. "I didn't know who you were."

Pumbaa, having just managed to free himself, sat panting on the ground.

"Oh. Pumbaa," said Simba, "this is Nala."

Pumbaa tried to catch his breath. "Pleased to meet you."

Nala smiled at the warthog. Then she grew serious. "Simba," she asked, "why would Scar tell us you were dead?"

"It doesn't matter," said Simba. "I'm alive."

"Of course it matters," said Nala. "You're the king."

Pumbaa dropped, at once, to his knees. "Your Majesty," he said. "I gravel at your feet."

"Get up," said Timon. "It's not *gravel*. It's *grovel*. And don't. Believe me, he's not the king."

"Tell him the truth, Simba," Nala urged him.

"Yeah, she's right," admitted Simba.

"Now everything's ruined!" cried Timon. "It'll never be the same around here."

Nala turned to Timon and Pumbaa. "Would you both excuse us for a little while? I'd like to talk to Simba alone."

"Sure," said Timon in a huff. "Come on, Pumbaa, let's give them a little privacy."

"I knew it!" said Pumbaa as they walked away. "I knew he was a king all along."

"Well, I'm surprised!" admitted Timon. "You think you know a guy. . . ."

* * *

"You never told them who you are?" asked Nala when they were by themselves.

"They never asked me," said Simba. "Look, enough about me. How did you get here?"

"Things are terrible at home," said Nala. "Scar has taken over. He lets the hyenas do whatever they want!"

Simba was shocked. "That sounds awful!" he said.

"With all the hyenas," Nala explained, "it got so bad I couldn't take it anymore, so I ran away. I guess I thought I'd find something better."

"And you did—me!" said Simba with a big grin. "Now we can have a great life together."

Nala smiled sadly. "It sounds perfect, Simba, but we can't. *We're* not all that matters. Now that we're together, we can go back to Pride Rock to set things right."

"Nala," Simba tried to explain, "I live by a new philosophy now. *Hakuna matata.* It means no cares, no worries, no responsibilities—"

"Listen to me!" interrupted Nala. "Forget this *hakuna matata* business. Accept your responsibilities, Simba. With you alive, Scar has no right to the throne."

Simba shook his head.

"Nala," he persisted. "I just can't go back. I'm no king."

"You could be," Nala told him.

Simba gazed deep into Nala's eyes. "I've missed you, Nala."

"I've missed you, too," Nala said.

"Let me show you around. I'm sure you'll get to like it here," he said. "Come on. *Please.*"

Nala followed him into the leafy sun-dappled jungle.

"It's beautiful," she gasped. "I can see why you like it. This whole place is like a paradise."

"I told you," said Simba, stretching out on a soft bed of moss. "This is all we need."

Nala walked away.

"Nala," said Simba, "there's one more place I want to show you. It's one of my favorite spots."

He took her to a little waterfall. In a rainbow mist, the waterdrops bounced and sparkled as they fell. Simba jumped into the icy pond.

"Come on in!" he called, slapping the water with his paw.

Nala hesitated, then laughed and joined him.

All afternoon they played hide-and-seek in the tumbling falls. When the air grew cool, they strolled to a hilltop and watched the sun set.

"Nala," Simba asked, nuzzling her. "Stay with me. Why go back to a world that's defeated us?"

Nala looked away. She couldn't stand to hear Simba talk like that. She couldn't believe Mufasa's son would turn his back on the pride.

"You're hiding from the future, Simba," she answered.

"It's too hard for me to give up what's here," said Simba. "You don't understand."

"Neither would your father. Mufasa would want you to go back," she told him.

Simba blinked back his tears. "My father is dead, and it's all my fault."

9

Simba couldn't sleep. His talk with Nala kept going around and around in his head. He looked over at her. She was sleeping quietly. Maybe he'd go for a little walk; it might make him drowsy.

The jungle was unusually quiet. He strolled for a few minutes, then stretched out on a flat rock and gazed at the sky. It was packed with stars.

I can't go back, he thought. How could I show my face in the pride? I'm no king. I can't right the wrongs of the world.

"And even if I tried," he sighed out loud, "I'm not you, Dad. I never will be."

Gradually Simba became aware of a faint sound—the sound of someone singing a strange little tune. *"Asante sana, squash banana. We we nugu, mi mi apana."* He strained to hear the words. He couldn't tell where they were coming from. Something about them was sad and disturbing, so he decided to move on.

In a little while he stopped to rest again. He

relaxed along a fallen log that bridged a narrow stream. *PLOPPP!* A stone thrown from the shore, narrowly missing his head, had landed in the water.

Startled and annoyed, Simba saw an old baboon squatting by the side of the stream. Rafiki grinned at Simba. *"Asante sana, squash banana. We we nugu, mi mi apana,"* he crooned.

"Are you following me?" asked Simba. "Who are you?"

Rafiki looked him in the eye. "The question is," he asked, "who are *you*?"

Simba sighed. "I thought I knew. Now I'm not so sure."

"Well," said Rafiki, "I do know who you are. You're Mufasa's boy.

"Bye now," he added, and scooted away through the underbrush.

Simba hardly believed what he'd just heard. The old baboon knew his father? He had to stop him before he got away.

"Wait!" shouted Simba. He charged through the vines and chased Rafiki up to the top of a rocky hill.

"You knew my father?" he asked him.

Rafiki shook his head. "Let me correct you," he said. "I *know* your father."

Simba felt sorry he had to give such bad news

to the old baboon. "I hate to tell you this," he said, "but my father died a long time ago."

"Let me correct you again," Rafiki said. "Your father is *alive*! You follow Rafiki. He knows the way."

Simba's heart swelled with hope. Rafiki's name stirred up long-ago memories of Pride Rock. Now, for the first time since he'd left home, he felt truly happy. He was going to see his father!

The old baboon was surprisingly quick, and it was hard to keep up with him. One second he'd be in sight, and the next he'd be gone, as if by magic. When Simba thought he'd lost track of Rafiki for good, he saw him beckoning.

"Hurry! Don't dawdle!" called out Rafiki. "Mufasa's waiting."

He led the way through more tangles and underbrush. At last he stopped near a deep pool screened by leafy plants and tall reeds.

"Is my father here?" asked Simba.

Rafiki hobbled up to the reeds and parted them.

"Shh," he murmured, putting a long bony finger to his gray lips. "Look down there."

Simba crept closer and looked into the still pool. The water sparkled with the reflection of the stars. Gazing at him, through the stars, was a lion with a golden mane.

"Dad?" asked Simba. As he leaned forward he realized it wasn't his father at all. He was just looking at himself. Overwhelmed with disappointment, he turned to Rafiki. Was the old baboon playing some kind of mean trick?

"That's not my father," Simba told him. "It's just my reflection."

"Look harder," said Rafiki.

Puzzled, Simba stared into the shining water again. His reflection shimmered and gradually changed shape. It was turning into his father's image!

Simba gasped.

"You see," said Rafiki, "he lives in you."

"Simba . . ."

Simba looked up. It was his father's voice!

"Dad, where are you?" he cried.

Before Simba's amazed eyes, a swirl of clouds parted, and Mufasa's image slowly filled the night sky. But it wasn't really his father—he could see right through him. Simba gulped. He was looking at a ghost!

"Dad?" he asked, beginning to feel afraid.

"Simba, have you forgotten me?" asked Mufasa.

"No!" cried Simba. How could his father ever think that?

The king's image changed again. Simba could

no longer see the ghost but instead could feel his father's presence all around him. Mufasa had become a part of the air itself.

"You have forgotten who you are," said the voice of Mufasa. *"And so, you have forgotten me."*

"Oh, no, Dad," insisted Simba. He felt a sob rising in his throat. "I'd never forget you."

Mufasa's voice grew gentle. *"Look inside yourself, Simba. You are more than what you have been. You must take your place in the Circle of Life."*

"But Dad, I've made a place for myself here," explained Simba. "I'm not who I used to be. How can I go back?"

"Remember who you are," said his father. *"You are my son and the one true king."*

Mufasa's voice started to fade.

"Remember who you are. . . ."

"Dad!" pleaded Simba. "Please don't go! Don't leave me!"

"Remember . . . remember . . . ," repeated the voice as it faded away.

"Dad?" Simba called faintly. Simba searched the huge starry sky, but Mufasa was gone.

"Most peculiar night, eh?" said Rafiki, who appeared beside Simba once again.

"Looks like the winds are changing," answered Simba.

"Ah," sighed Rafiki. "Change is good."

"But it's not easy," said Simba. "I know I have to go back, but going back means I have to face my past."

Just then Rafiki smacked Simba with his walking stick.

"Ouch!" yelled Simba. "What'd you do that for?"

"It doesn't matter," said Rafiki. "It's in the past already."

"Yeah, but it still hurts," said Simba, rubbing his head.

"Yes, the past can hurt," said Rafiki. "The way I see it, you can either learn from the pain or run from it." Rafiki suddenly raised his stick again, only this time, Simba ducked away.

"Now you're learning!" said Rafiki. "So what are you going to do?"

"First I'm going to take your stick!" said Simba. "And then I'm going back home."

* * *

Just before dawn, Nala's voice woke Pumbaa and Timon.

"I was calling for Simba," she told them. "Is he here?"

Timon looked surprised. "We thought he was with you."

"Where'd he go?" asked Pumbaa.

"I don't know," explained Nala. "When did you see him last?"

54

"When he was with you!" said Timon.

"Ha-ha," interrupted Rafiki, squatting on an overhead tree limb. "You won't find him here. The king has returned."

Hearing the old baboon's words, Nala roared in delight. "He's really gone back!" She watched Rafiki quickly disappear into the trees. I was wrong about Simba, she thought.

"What's goin' on here?" demanded Timon. "Who's the monkey?"

"Simba's gone back to challenge Scar," said Nala.

"Who's got a scar?" asked Pumbaa.

"No, no, no," said Nala. "It's his uncle."

Timon was amazed. "The monkey's his uncle?"

"No," explained Nala slowly. "Simba's gone back to challenge his uncle and to take his place as king."

"Ohhhh," said Timon and Pumbaa together.

Timon thought it over. "A challenge?" he asked in a worried voice. "You mean it might be a fight— to the death?"

Nala nodded sadly.

Pumbaa gasped. "Simba might be killed!"

"*You!*" Timon yelled at Nala. "This is because of *you*!"

"You don't understand, Timon," said Nala.

"I don't understand?" squealed Timon. "*You*

don't understand. Simba's marchin' off into the jaws of death, and it's all your fault."

He began to sob. Nala turned to leave.

"Hey," said Timon, looking up. "Where're you goin'?"

"I'm going with Simba," said Nala.

"I'm going, too," said Pumbaa. "Like Simba, who marches off into the face of death, I, too, go to meet my destiny . . . as his faithful friend."

"Fine!" yelled Timon. "Go! Be a hero. Who needs you here, anyway. Now *I'm* king of the jungle!"

Timon stood with his arms crossed for a moment or two. Then he dashed after them.

"Hey, you guys," he yelled. "Wait for me!"

10

Simba reached the top of a high plateau. At last he'd reached the edge of the Pride Lands. Pride Rock stood tall in the middle of the empty, parched plain.

Everything had been touched by the drought. The trees were almost leafless. Starving giraffes, stretching as high as possible, had eaten the branches bare. The enormous ancient baobabs were stripped, their stringy bark devoured by desperate, hungry elephants.

The dry wind picked up, and threatening clouds gathered overhead. Perhaps they were bringing rain! As the wind blew his mane, Simba breathed deeply and closed his eyes. He thought of his father's words. *Remember . . . remember . . .*

Then he went down into the Pride Lands.

* * *

Inside Scar's cave, Zazu was cooped up in a cage, humming mournfully to himself.

"Sing something with a little bounce to it!" Scar ordered.

"I would never be treated like this by Mufasa," said Zazu.

"*What* did you say?" Scar exploded. "You are never ever to say that name in my presence. I am the king!"

"Yes, sire," Zazu said meekly. And then more boldly he said, "Only *you* could rule the pride as only you do."

Just then Shenzi, Banzai, and Ed burst into the cave.

"You gotta do something, boss," yowled Shenzi. "It's dinnertime, and we're out of entrees."

"Yeah—and there's no food, either," cried Banzai.

"The hyenas are so hungry they're ready to riot!" said Shenzi.

"It's the lionesses' job to hunt for food," snarled Scar. "Must I do everything!"

He poked his head out of the cave. "Saar-ra-bee!" he roared.

* * *

A few minutes later Sarabi arrived.

"Listen to all those hungry stomachs out there," Scar told her.

"Scar," said Sarabi, "there's no food—the herds have moved on. We have no choice. We must leave Pride Rock."

"We're not going anywhere," said Scar. "I'm king and I make the rules!"

"If you were half the king Mufasa was—," began Sarabi.

"I AM TEN TIMES THE KING MUFASA WAS!" roared Scar, and with a powerful swipe of his paw, he knocked Sarabi to the ground.

The other animals fell silent as lightning flashed in the dark sky. High above the plain, storm clouds began to churn. Thunder boomed. The wind howled and roared. *Zaapp!* A blinding lightning bolt scorched the earth, and the dry grasses caught fire. Swirling flames swept toward Pride Rock.

Staring into the smoky air, Scar gasped. Appearing in the smoky haze like a ghost, a golden-maned lion approached him.

"Mufasa? No! It can't be!" he said, backing up. "You're dead!"

Sarabi raised her aching head. "Mufasa?" she asked.

"No, Mother," said Simba. "It's me."

"Simba . . . you're alive," said Sarabi weakly.

"Simba?" whispered Scar. Then he quickly recovered from his shock. "Well, Simba. I'm surprised to see you. Stroke of bad timing, your showing up when you did."

"I'd say I'm right on time," said Simba.

"Well, you know," Scar stumbled, "the pressures of ruling a kingdom—"

"Are no longer yours," finished Simba. "I've come back to take my place as king."

"Sorry, Nephew," Scar said, "but there are some who still think I'm king." He nodded to the throng of hyenas poised for attack.

Simba saw Nala and the other lionesses on a ledge above, ready to spring to his aid. "Step down or fight, Scar," Simba yelled.

"Must we be violent? Your father isn't here to save you this time," said Scar. "Why don't you tell them who's responsible for your father's death."

Sorrow flooded Simba's heart. He took a step back and said softly, "I am."

The crowd of lionesses gasped.

"But it was an accident!"

"You're guilty!" said Scar.

"Noooo!" Simba backed away in horror and suddenly stumbled, his hind legs slipping off the back of a steep cliff.

"Simba!" cried Nala.

Scar slowly walked to the edge of the cliff and peered at Simba. Digging his claws into the rock, Simba barely held on.

"Now *this* looks familiar," Scar mumbled. "Oh yes. I remember! This is just the way your father looked—before I killed him!"

The words struck Simba with the force of a blow. A new strength surged through his body and with an explosive roar he lunged at Scar. "Murderer!" he cried out.

Gripping Scar's throat, he turned toward the pride. "Tell them what you just said, Scar," yelled Simba. "Tell them the truth."

"Truth?" Scar questioned. "Truth is in the eye of the beholder."

Simba tightened his grasp around Scar's throat. "Tell them!"

"I did it," whispered Scar, barely able to breathe.

"Say it louder," cried Simba.

"I killed Mufasa!" Scar yelled.

With ear-piercing battle cries, the lionesses lunged at Scar. Simba saw Nala spring to his side just as the hyenas charged into the fray. Throughout the fighting, lightning flashed, and the dry grass below Pride Rock turned into a sea of flames, filling the air with choking smoke and ash.

Finally, the hyenas fled in defeat, leaving Simba and Scar face-to-face.

"Please, don't hurt me," pleaded Scar. He had no one to help him. His back was to the cliff. "I didn't kill your father. It was the hyenas. They're evil. Simba, I'm your family."

Simba paused briefly, considering his uncle's plea. "Run away, Scar," Simba ordered. "Go—and never show your face again."

"Y-yes, Your Majesty. As you wish," Scar said,

pretending to leave. Then, snarling, he spun around and struck out at his nephew.

Simba moved quickly. "You've lost your chance!" he roared.

He grabbed Scar and heaved him over the edge.

At the bottom, the waiting pack of starving hyenas threw themselves upon him. The hyenas' eerie laughter echoed all around. Scar was no longer their master, and within minutes he was no more.

Above, Simba felt someone at his side.

"Welcome home," Nala said. "Your mother is waiting to greet the new king. . . ."

Simba nuzzled her. "It's good to be back."

"That was quite a battle," said Nala. "Timon even came to the rescue. He and Pumbaa got rid of Shenzi, Banzai, and Ed."

Simba smiled. "And how's Zazu?"

"Fine," Nala quipped. "He's free as a bird."

As they smiled at each other, it started to rain. The pounding drops put out the fire and soaked the black, smoky ground. Within minutes sheets of water drenched the plain, and gurgling streams snaked across the land once again.

The Pride Lands came back to life. The water holes overflowed, and the grasses grew green and tall. Acacia trees, their branches heavy with tiny golden puffballs, scented the air. The kigelia trees bloomed all around. At night, when the flowers opened, fruit bats drank the nectar.

One dawn all the animals journeyed to the foot of Pride Rock. Zazu circled low above them and then flew out of sight.

"Why are we here?" a young zebra wanted to know.

"Be patient," said his father. "Soon you will see the little prince. Look! There he is now!"

On top of Pride Rock, Timon and Pumbaa sat amid a group of lionesses. They watched as the strange old baboon sprinkled something over the little cub's head. The cub sneezed, and everyone laughed.

Rafiki picked up the wiggling cub and moved to the edge. At once everyone cheered and stamped their feet.

Then Rafiki raised the cub—the son of King

Simba and Queen Nala—high in the air.

The animals fell silent and bowed to their future king.

* * *

After the crowd had gone, Simba stood at the top of Pride Rock. He watched the sun set beyond the western hills. It was evening once again in Africa.

"Everything is all right, Dad," Simba said softly. "You see, I remembered. . . ." He gazed upward. One by one each star took its place in the cold night sky.